Richard Hovey

**Seaward**

an elegy on the death of Thomas William Parsons

Richard Hovey

**Seaward**

*an elegy on the death of Thomas William Parsons*

ISBN/EAN: 9783337387792

Printed in Europe, USA, Canada, Australia, Japan

Cover: Foto ©Andreas Hilbeck / pixelio.de

More available books at **www.hansebooks.com**

T. W. Parkons

# SEAWARD

*AN ELEGY ON THE DEATH OF*
*THOMAS WILLIAM PARSONS*

BY

## RICHARD HOVEY

BOSTON
D. LOTHROP COMPANY
1893

"*Il tremolar della marina.*" —DANTE.

*Looking seaward well assured*
*That the word the vessel brings*
*Is the word they wish to hear.*

— EMERSON.


*There is a city builded by no hand,*
  *And unapproachable by any shore,*
*And unassailable by any band*
  *Of storming soldiery forevermore.*

— PARSONS.

# SEAWARD

# SEAWARD

---

## I.

THE tide is in the marshes.  Far
away
In Nova Scotia's woods
they follow me,
Marshes of distant Massa-
chusetts Bay,
Dear marshes, where the
dead once loved to be !
I see them lying  yellow in
the sun,
And hear the mighty tremor of the sea
Beyond the dunes where blue cloud-shadows run.

## II.

KNOW that there the tide is
    coming in,
    Secret and slow, for in my
      heart I feel
The silent swelling of a stress
    akin;
    And in my vision, lo! blue
      glimpses steal
Across the yellow marsh-grass,
    where the flood,
  Filling the empty channels, lifts the keel
Of one lone cat-boat bedded in the mud.

## III.

The tide is in the marshes.   Kingscroft fades;
  It is not Minas there across the lea;
But I am standing under pilgrim shades
  Far off where Scituate lapses to the sea.
And he, my elder brother in the muse,
  The poet of the Charles and Italy,
Stands by my side, Song's gentle, shy recluse.

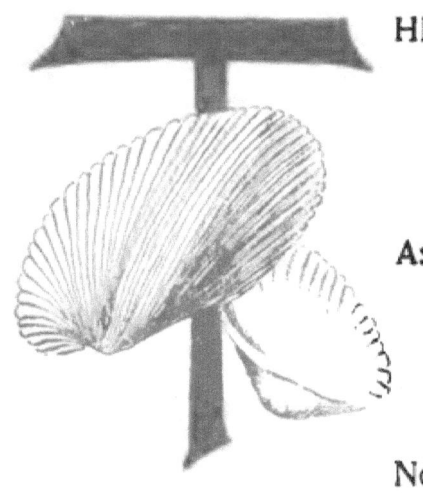

THE hermit thrush of singers, few might draw
  So near his ambush in the solitude
  As to be witness of the holy awe
  And passionate sweetness of his singing mood.
  Not oft he sang, and then in ways apart,
Where foppish ignorance might not intrude
To mar the joy of his sufficing art.


V.


Only for love of song he sang, unbid
  And unexpectant of responsive praise;
But they that loved and sought him where he hid,
  Forbearing to profane his templed ways,
Went marveling if that clear voice they heard
  Pass thrilling through the hushed religious maze,
Were of a spirit singing or a bird.

ALAS! he is not here, he
will not sing;
The air is empty of him ever-
more.
Alone I watch the slow kelp-
gatherers bring
Their dories full of sea-moss to
the shore.
No gentle eyes look out to sea with mine,
No gentle lips are uttering quaint lore,
No hand is on my shoulder for a sign.

## VII.

Far, far, so far, the crying of the surf!
Still, still, so still, the water in the grass!
Here on the knoll the crickets in the turf
And one bold squirrel barking, seek, alas!
To bring the swarming summer back to me.
In vain; my heart is on the salt morass
Below, that stretches to the sunlit sea.

INTERMINABLE, not to be
divined,
The ocean's solemn dis-
tances recede;
A gospel of glad color to
the mind,
But for the soul a voice of
sterner creed.

The sadness of unfathomable things
   Calls from the waste and makes the heart give heed
With answering dirges, as a seashell sings.

IX.

Mother of infinite loss! Mother bereft!
   Thou of the shaken hair! Far-questing Sea!
Sea of the lapsing wail of waves! O left
   Of many lovers! Lone, lamenting Sea!
Desolate, prone, disheveled, lost, sublime!
   Unquelled and reckless! Mad, despairing Sea!
Wail, for I wait — wail, ancient dirge of Time!

## X.

O more, no more
that brow to greet,
no more!
Mourn, bitter heart! mourn,
fool of Fate! Again
Thy lover leaves thee; from thy
pleading shore
Swept far beyond the caverns
of the rain,
No phantom of him lingers on the air.
Thy foamy fingers reach for his — in vain!
In vain thy salt breath searches for his hair!


## XI.

Mourn gently, tranquil marshes, mourn with me!
Mourn, if acceptance so serene can mourn!
Grieve, marshes, though your noonday melody
Of color thrill through sorrow like a horn
Blown far in Elfland! Mourn, free-wandering dunes!
For he has left you of his voice forlorn,
Who sang your slopes full of an hundred Junes.

VIKING Death,
what hast thou
done with him?
Sea-wolf of Fate, marau-
der of the shore!
Storm-reveler, to what ca-
rousal grim
Hast thou compelled him? Hark!
through the Sea's roar
Heroic laughter mocking us afar!
There will no answer come forevermore,
Though for his sake Song beacon to a star.

Mourn, Muse beyond the sea! Ausonian Muse!
Mourn, where thy vinelands watch the day depart!
Mourn for him, where thy sunsets interfuse,
Who loved thy beauty with no alien heart,
And sang it in his not all alien line!
Muse of the passionate thought and austere art!
O Dante's Muse! lament his son and thine.

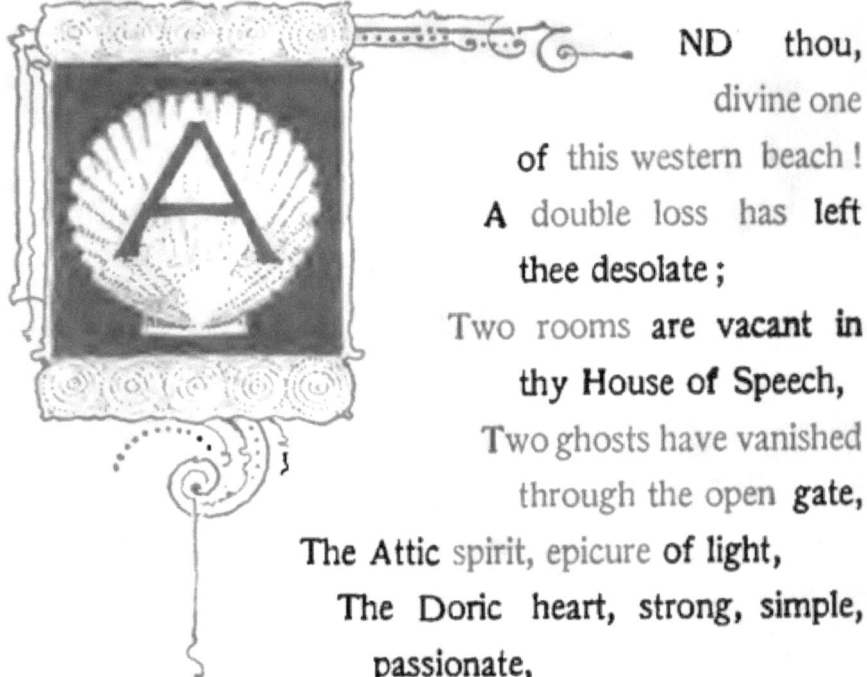

ND thou,
divine one
of this western beach!
A double loss has left
thee desolate;
Two rooms are vacant in
thy House of Speech,
Two ghosts have vanished
through the open gate,
The Attic spirit, epicure of light,
The Doric heart, strong, simple,
passionate,
Thy priest of Beauty, and thy priest of Right.

## XV.

Last of the elder choir save one whose smile
Is gentler for its memories, they rest.
Mourn, goddess, come apart and mourn awhile.
Come with thy sons, lithe Song-Queen of the
West —
The poet Friend of Poets, the great throng
Of seekers on the long elusive quest,
And the lone voice of Arizonian song.

## XVI.

NOR absent they, thy latest-
born, O Muse,
My young companions in Art's
wildwood ways;
She whose swift verse speaks
words that smite and bruise
With scarlet suddenness of flaming
phrase,
Virginia's hawk of Song; and he who
sings
Alike his people's homely rustic lays
And his fine spirit's high imaginings,


## XVII.

Far-stretching Indiana's melodist,
Quaint, humorous, full of quirks and wanton whims,
Full-throated, with imagination kissed;
With these, two pilgrims from auroral streams,
The Greek revealer of Canadian skies
And thy close darling, voyager of dreams,
Carman, the sweetest, strangest voice that cries.

## XVIII.

ND thou, friend of my
heart, in fireside bonds
Near to the dead, not with
the poet's bay
Brow-bound but eminent with
kindred fronds,
Paint us some picture of the
summer day
For his memorial — the distant
dune,
The marshes stretching palpitant away
And blue sea fervid with the stress of noon.

## XIX.

For we were of the few who knew his face,
Nor only heard the rumor of his fame;
This house beside the sea the sacred place
Where first with thee to clasp his hand I came —
Art's knight of courtesy, well-pleased to commend
Who to my youth accorded the dear name
Of poet, and the dearer name of friend.

## XX.

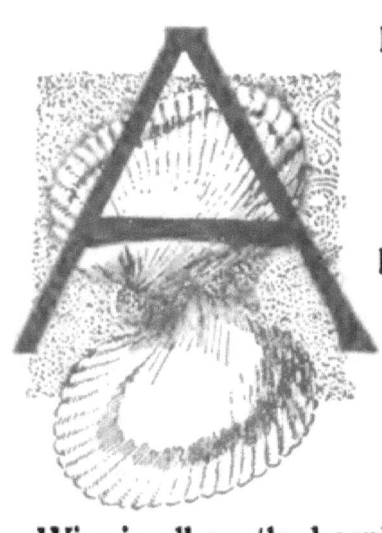

H, that last bottle of old Gas-
con wine
We drank together! I re-
member too
How carefully he placed it
where the shine
Of the warm sun might
pierce it through and
through —
Wise in all gentle, hospitable arts —
And there was sunshine in it when we drew
The cork and drank, and sunshine in our hearts.


## XXI.

O mourners by the sea, who loved him most!
I watch you where you move, I see you all;
Unmarked I glide among you like a ghost,
And on the portico, in room and hall,
Lay visionary fingers on your hair.
You do not feel their unsubstantial fall
Nor hear my silent tread, but I am there.

## XXII.

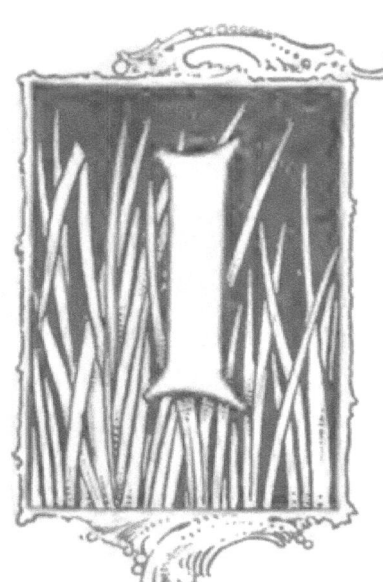

**I** WOULD my thought had but the weakest throat,

To set the air a-vibrate with a word.

Alas ! dumb, ineffectual, remote,

I murmur, but my solace is not heard ;

Nor, could I reach you, would your grief abate.

What sorrow ever was with speech deterred ?

What power has Song against the hand of Fate ?. . .

## XXIII.

Not all in vain ! For with the will to serve,

Myself am served, at least. A secure calm

Soars in my soul with wings that will not swerve,

And on my brow I feel a ministering palm.

Even in the effort for another's peace

I have achieved mine own. I hear a psalm

Of angels. and the grim forebodings cease.

## XXIV.

I SEE things as they are,
      nor longer yield
  To truce and parley with the
    doubts of sense.
My certainty of vision goes
    a-field,
    Wide-ranging, fearless, into
      the immense;
  And finds no terror there, no
    ghost nor ghoul,
Not to be dazzled back to impotence,
Confronted with the indomitable soul.

## XXV.

What goblin frights us?  Are we children, then,
  To start at shadows?  Things fantastic slay
The imperishable spirit in whose ken
  Their only birth is?  Blaze one solar ray
Across the grisly darkness that appals,
  And where the gloom was murkiest, the bright Day
Laughs with a light of blosmy coronals.

## XXVI.

TRETCH wide, O
marshes, in your golden joy!
Stretch ample, marshes, in
serene delight!
Proclaiming faith past tempest
to destroy,
With silent confidence of con-
scious might!
Glad of the blue sky, knowing nor wind nor rain
Can do your large indifference despite,
Nor lightning mar your tolerant disdain!


## XXVII.

The fanfare of the trumpets of the sea
Assaults the air with jubilant foray;
The intolerable exigence of glee
Shouts to the sun and leaps in radiant spray;
The laughter of the breakers on the shore
Shakes like the mirth of Titans heard at play,
With thunders of tumultuous uproar.

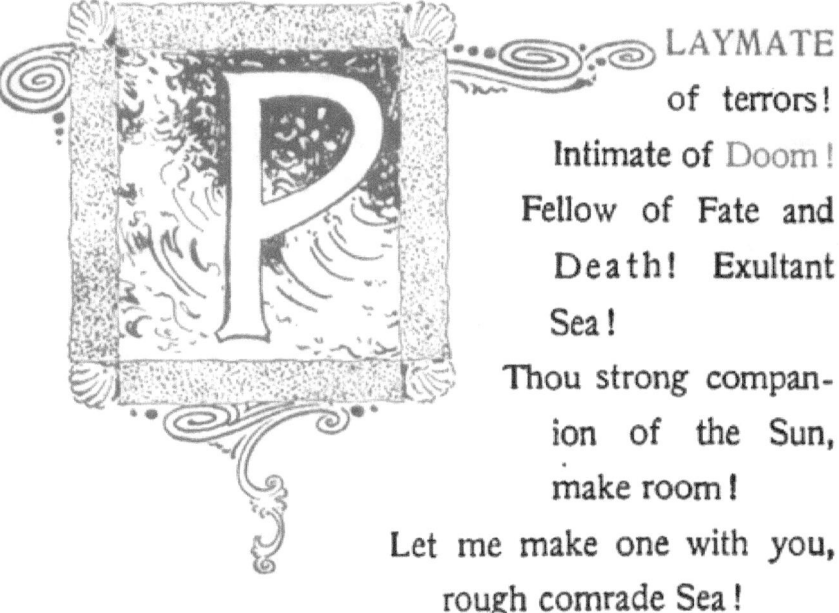

LAYMATE
of terrors!
Intimate of Doom!
Fellow of Fate and
Death! Exultant
Sea!
Thou strong compan-
ion of the Sun,
make room!
Let me make one with you,
rough comrade Sea!
Sea of the boisterous sport of wind and spray!
Sea of the lion mirth! Sonorous Sea!
I hear thy shout, I know what thou wouldst say.

## XXIX.

Dauntless, triumphant, reckless of alarms,
O Queen that laughest Time and Fear to scorn,
Death, like a bridegroom, tosses in thine arms.
The rapture of your fellowship is borne
Like music on the wind. I hear the blare,
The calling of the undesisting horn,
And tremors as of trumpets on the air.

EA-CAPTAIN of whose keels the
the Sea is fain,
    Death, Master of a thousand ships,
    each prow
That sets against the thunders of the
main
    Is lyric with thy mirth.  I know
    thee now,
O Death, I shout back to thy hearty hail,
    Thou of the great heart and the cavernous brow,
Strong Seaman at whose look the north winds quail.

Poet, thou hast adventured in the roar
    Of mighty seas with one that never failed
To make the havens of the further shore.
    Beyond that vaster Ocean thou hast sailed
What old immortal world of beauty lies!
    What land where light for matter has prevailed!
What strange Atlantid dream of Paradise!

OWN what dim bank
of violets did he come,
The mild historian of the
Sudbury Inn,
Welcoming thee to that long-
wished-for home?
What talk of comrades old didst thou
begin?
What dear inquiry lingered on his tongue
Of the Sicilian, ere he led thee in
To the eternal company of Song?


## XXXIII.


There thy co-laborers and high compeers
Hailed thee as courtly hosts some noble guest —
Poe, disengloomed with the celestial years,
Calm Bryant, Emerson of the antique zest
And modern vision, Lowell all a-bloom
At last, unwintered of his mind's unrest,
And Walt, old Walt, with the old superb aplomb.

OT far from these Lanier, deplored
  so oft
    From Georgian live-oaks to Aca-
    dian firs,
  Walks with his friend as once at
    Cedarcroft.
    And many more I see of speech
    diverse;
  From whom a band aloof and sep-
    arate,
    Landor and Meleager in converse,
And lonely Collins, for thy greeting wait.

## XXXV.

But who is this that from the mightier shades
  Emerges, seeing whose sacred laureate hair
Thou startest forward trembling through the glades,
  Advancing upturned palms of filial prayer?
Long hast thou served him; now, of lineament
  Not stern but strenuous still, thy pious care
He comes to guerdon.   Art thou not content?

## XXXVI.

FORBEAR, O Muse, to
sing his deeper bliss,
What tenderer meetings,
what more secret joys!
Lift not the veil of hea-
venly privacies!
Suffice it that nought unful-
filled alloys
The pure gold of the rapture of
his rest,
Save that some linger where the jarring noise
Of earth afflicts, whom living he caressed.


## XXXVII.

His feet are in thy courts, O Lord; his ways
Are in the City of the Living God.
Beside the eternal sources of the days
He dwells, his thoughts with timeless lightnings shod;
His hours are exaltations and desires,
The soul itself its only period,
And life unmeasured save as it aspires.

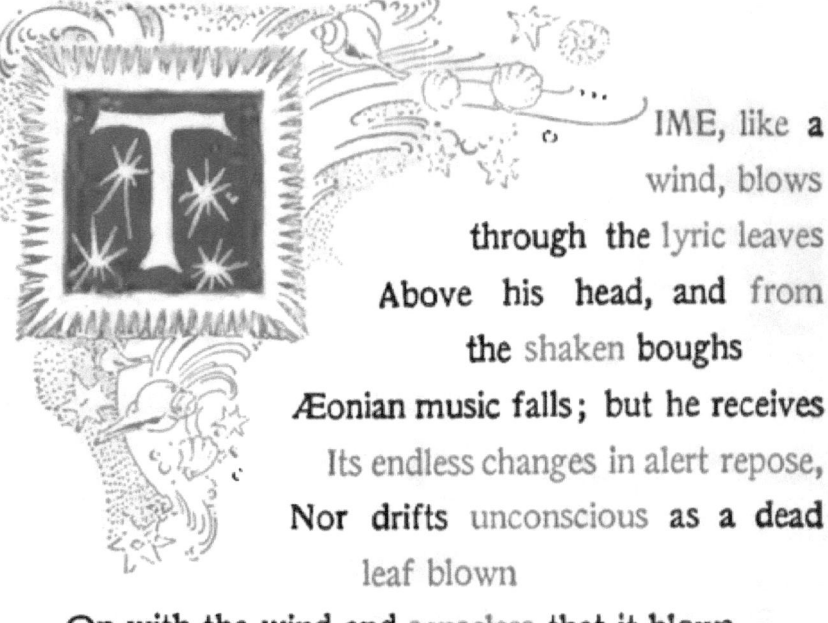

IME, like a
wind, blows
through the lyric leaves
Above his head, and from
the shaken boughs
Æonian music falls; but he receives
Its endless changes in alert repose,
Nor drifts unconscious as a dead
leaf blown
On with the wind and senseless that it blows,
But hears the chords like armies marching on.

## XXXIX.

About his paths the tall swift angels are,
Whose motion is like music but more sweet;
The centuries for him their gates unbar;
He hears the stars their *Glorias* repeat;
And in high moments when the fervid soul
Burns white with love, lo! on his gaze replete
The Vision of the Godhead shall unroll —

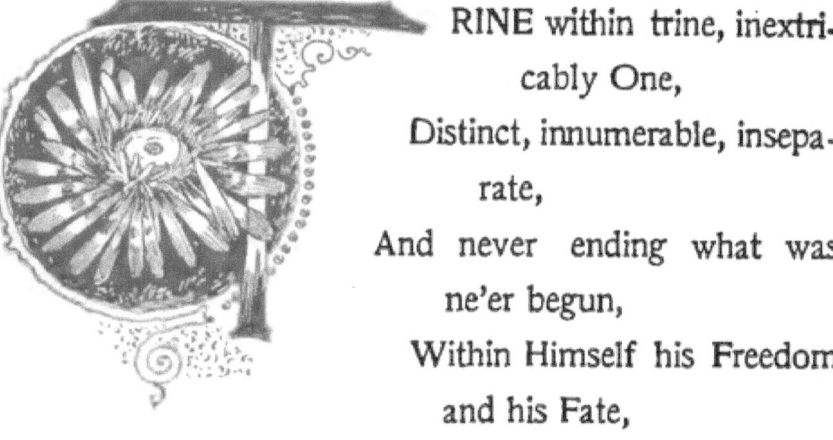

TRINE within trine, inextri-
cably One,
Distinct, innumerable, insepa-
rate,
And never ending what was
ne'er begun,
Within Himself his Freedom
and his Fate,
All dreams, all harmonies, all Forms of light
In his Infinity intrinsecate —
Until the soul no more can bear the sight.

## XLI.

O secret taciturn disdainful Death!
Knowing all this, why hast thou held thy peace?
Master of Silence, thou wilt waste no breath
On weaklings, nor to stiffen nerveless knees
Deny strong men the conquest of one qualm —
And they, thy dauntless comrades, are at ease,
And need no speech, and greet thee calm for calm.

## XLII.

AST them adrift in wastes
of ageless Night,
Or bid them follow into
Hell, they dare;
So are they worthy of their
thrones of light.
O that great tranquil
rapture they shall share!
That life compact of adamantine fire!
My soul goes out across the eastern air
To that far country with a wild desire! . . .

## XLIII.

But still the marshes haunt me; still my thought
Returns upon their silence, there to brood
Till the significance of earth is brought
Back to my heart, and in a sturdier mood
I turn my eyes toward the distance dim,
And in the purple far infinitude
Watch the white ships sink under the sea-rim;

OME bound for Flemish
    ports or Genovese,
  Some for Bermuda bound,
    or Baltimore ;
Others, perchance, for fur-
    ther Orient seas,
  Sumatra and the straits of
    Singapore,
Or antique cities of remote
    Cathay,
Or past Gibraltar and the Libyan shore,
Through Bab-el-mandeb eastward to Bombay ;


XLV.


And one shall signal flaming Teneriffe,
  And the Great Captive's ocean-prison speak,
Then on beyond the demon-haunted cliff,
  By Madagascar's palms and Mozambique,
Till in some sudden tropic dawn afar
  The Sultan sees the colors at her peak
Salute the minarets of Zanzibar.

# NOTES

# NOTES.

---

## THOMAS WILLIAM PARSONS.

The subject of this elegy was born at Boston in 1819, and educated at the Boston Latin School. While yet a young man he visited England and Italy, with which latter country and its literature his life was to be so largely occupied. From early youth he was a devoted student of Dante, to the translation of whose " Divine Comedy" he chiefly applied his scholarship and poetic genius. In 1854 he published a volume of original poems, among which were the famous verses, " On a Bust of Dante," which found their way at once into all the anthologies. Several other volumes were privately printed, and in 1892 he published " Circum Præcordia," which contained, besides a versification of the collects of the Church as set forth in the Book of Common Prayer, about a dozen original poems of a religious nature. The translation of the first ten cantos of the " Inferno " was published in 1843, and the complete " Inferno" in 1867. The opening cantos of the " Purgatorio " were issued in 1876, and the remaining cantos were afterward completed and are now in process of publication. In 1870 Mr. Parsons was made a Corresponding Fellow of the Reale Accademia de' Fisiocritici in Siena. He died at Scituate, Mass., September 3, 1892.

"Dr. Parsons holds a place of his own. He is one of those rare poets whose infrequent work is so beautiful as to make us wish for more. In quality, at least, it is of a kind with Landor's; his touch is sure, and has at command the choicer modes of lyrical art — those which, although fashion may overslaugh them, return again, and enable a true poet to be quite as original as when hunting devices previously unessayed. His independence on the other hand, is exhibited in his free renderings of Dante. . . . .

"Parsons's briefer poems often are models, but occasionally show a trace of that stiffness which too little employment gives even the hand of daintier sense. 'Lines on a Bust of Dante,' in structure, diction, loftiness of thought, is the peer of any modern lyric in our tongue. Inversion, the vice of stilted poets, becomes with him an excellence, and old forms and accents are rehandled and charged with life anew. It is to be regretted that Dr. Parsons has not used his gift more freely. He has been a poet for poets, rather than for the people; but many types are required to fill out the hemicycle of a nation's literature."

— *Stedman's Poets of America.*

"The study of a great man is an education. Dr. Parsons has been an unwearied student of Dante for thirty years [1869], and has reaped commensurate benefits from the familiarity. His lines to the immortal Florentine, by common consent, are ranked with the very noblest efforts of the American Muse. Among the other traits in the matchless style of Dante, are his unique conciseness and precision. His descriptions are coined rather than painted; his metaphors are not pictures, but medallions. This artistic horror of slovenly work, this conscientious finish of severe simplicity and force, the apt pupil shares with the great master."

—W. R. ALGER.

"He occupies some such place in American poetry as Gray or Collins does in English poetry, not having written much, but extremely well. The poet is not living in the country who could have written a stronger, grander poem than that on the 'Bust of Dante,' beginning:

'See, from this counterfeit of him
  Whom Arno shall remember long,
How stern of lineament, how grim,
  The father was of Tuscan song.'"

— WM. HAYES WARD.

---

### STANZA I.

#### "*In Nova Scotia's woods.*"

This poem was written in Windsor, Nova Scotia, at Kingscroft, the residence of Mr. Charles G. D. Roberts, where the author was staying when the news of the poet's death reached him. Kingscroft is situated on the edge of a beautiful wood of great fir-trees on an elevation overlooking the Avon River and the Basin of Minas.

### STANZA III.

#### "*Far off where Scituate lapses to the sea.*"

Scituate, where the poet died, is a village lying midway between Boston and Plymouth on that part of the coast of Massachusetts which is known as the South Shore. The country is of a gently undulating character, and the view seaward is across salt marshes broken here and there with low hillocks of a sandy formation.

### STANZA XIV.

#### "*A double loss.*"

The poet WHITTIER died but a few days after the death of Parsons.

### STANZA XV.

. . .   "*save one whose smile
  Is gentler for its memories,*"

OLIVER WENDELL HOLMES.

"*The poet Friend of Poets,*"

EDMUND CLARENCE STEDMAN.

Whittier, in dedicating one of his volumes to Stedman, called him "Poet, and Friend of Poets."

"*And the lone voice of Arizonian song,*"

JOAQUIN MILLER.

### STANZA XVI.

" *She whose swift verse,*" etc.,
AMELIE RIVES CHANLER.

### STANZA XVII.

" *Far-stretching Indiana's melodist,*
JAMES WHITCOMB RILEY.

" *The Greek revealer of Canadian skies,*
CHARLES G. D. ROBERTS.

### STANZA XVIII.

   . . . " *in fireside bonds*
*Near to the dead,*"

THOMAS BUFORD METEYARD, the painter, a relation of
Dr. Parsons.

### STANZA XXXII.

" *The mild historian of the Sudbury Inn,*"

LONGFELLOW. The old tavern at Sudbury was the scene
of "The Tales of a Wayside Inn." Parsons was the original of the Poet in that volume, and his brother-in-law, Luigi
Monti, of the Sicilian, to whom allusion is also made in this
stanza.

### STANZA XXXIV.

   . . . " *as once at Cedarcroft.*"

The home of Bayard Taylor, between whom and Lanier an
intimate bond of friendship existed.

### STANZA XXXV.

" *But who is this, that from the mightier shades*
  *Emerges,*"
DANTE.

   . . . " *now, of lineament*
*Not stern but strenuous still,*"

refers to Parsons's lines;

      " How stern of lineament, how grim
      The father was of Tuscan song."

*" Time, like a wind, blows through the lyric leaves*
*Above his head, and from the shaken boughs*
*Æonian music falls ; "*

'ἀμφὶ δὲ ψῦχρον κελάδει δι' ὕσδων
μαλίνων, αἰθυσσομένων δὲ φύλλων
κῶμα καταρρεῖ.

SAPPHO.

STANZA XLV.

. . . *" the demon-haunted cliff."*

The Cape of Good Hope, originally called the Cape of
Tempests. It is here that the spectral ship of Vanderdecken
is supposed to be seen in stormy weather, still battling
against the insuperable wind. Vanderdecken, the " Flying
Dutchman," tried to double the cape in spite of a heavy gale.
Baffled again and again, he swore that he would carry out
his purpose in spite of God or the Devil, though he had to
sail till the Day of Judgment. For this blasphemy he was
doomed to be taken at his word, and became a sort of Ahas-
uerus of the sea. This cape is also the scene of that tremen-
dous passage in the " Lusiad," where the giant, Adamastor,
appears in cloud and storm to the adventurous Portuguese
sailors, and warns them back from their enterprise:

" Não acabava, quando uma figura
Se nos mostra no ar, robusta e válida,
De disforme e grandissima estatura,
O rosto carregado, a barba esquálida :
Os olhos encovados, e a postura
Medonha e má, e a côr terrena e pállida ;
Cheios de terra, e crespos os cabellos,
A bocca negra, os dentes amarellos.

" Tam grande era de membros, que bem posso
Certificar-te, que este era o segundo
De Rhodes estranhissimo colosso,
Que um dos sete milagres foi do mundo :
C' um tom de voz nos falla horrendo e grosso,
Que pareceu sair do mar profundo :
Arripiam-se as carnes, e o cabello
A mi, e a todos, so de ouvil-o, e vella.

&ast;  &ast;  &ast;      &ast;     &ast;

" Mais ía per diante o monstro horrendo
Dizendo nossos fados, quando alçado
Lhe disse eu : 'Quem es tu? que esse estupendo
Corpo, certo me tem maravilhado.''
A bocca, e os olhos negros retorcendo,
E dando um espantoso e grande brado,
Me respondeu com voz pesada e amara,
Como quem da pergunta lhe pezara :

"'Eu sou aquelle occulto e grande cabo,
A quem chamais vós outros Tormentorio;
Que nunca a Tolomeu, Pomponio, Estrabo,
Plinio, e quantos passaram, fui notorio
Aqui toda a africana costa acabo
N' este meu nunca visto promontorio,
Que pera o pólo antárctico se estende,
A quem vossa ousadia tanto offende.

"Fui dos filhos aspérrimos da terra,
Qual Encélado, Egeu, e o Centimano;
Chamei-me Adamastor; e fui na guerra
Contra o que vibra os raios de Vulcano:
Não que puzesse serra sôbra serra;
Mas conquistando as ondas do Oceano,
Fui capitão do mar, per onde andava
A armada de Neptuno, que eu buscava.'"

—CAMOENS.

# A STUDY

# THOMAS WILLIAM PARSONS.

THE greatest achievements in poetry have been made by men who lived close to their times, and who responded easily to their environment. Not that Taine was altogether right in his climatic theory. The individual counts for much, and his output is really the result of the combined action of two influences, his personality and his surroundings — a sort of intellectual parallelogram of forces. Nor is great poetic accomplishment necessarily a sympathetic expression of contemporary tendencies. On the contrary, it may often antagonize them. But whether it antagonize or approve, it it is apt to be vitally related to them. No man ever set his face more strenuously against the trend of his age than Dante, nor denounced its manners and morals more severely; yet Dante was directly concerned in the practical affairs of his day, and his epoch is epitomized in his poems. Of course, great poetry bases itself below the shifting surfaces of eras and nationalities upon the immovable bed-rock of our common humanity; and so the greatest poets, the poets who express life most fundamentally, come to have a certain likeness to one another, even though they be as widely separated in time and space as Homer and Shakspere. But the poet must learn his human lesson at first hand; he must find the essential realities of life where he can see them with his own eyes, under the transitory garments which they wear in his day; and to do this he must be interested in his day.

There have been now and again, however, certain poets

who seem to have been born out of due time. They have not been opposed to their age so much as apart from it. The Hamlets of verse, for them the time has been out of joint, and they have not had the intensity or the resolution to strive to set it right. Thrown back upon themselves by an environment which was distasteful to them, but which they lacked either the force or the inclination to wrestle with and overcome, they have necessarily had little to say. But on that very account they have frequently given more thought to the purely artistic side of their work than more copious writers. Such men were Collins and Gray, and afterward Landor; men whom we admire more for the classic beauty of their style and for other technical qualities than for the scope of their imagination or the penetration of their insight. Of this class of poets, and with no mean rank among them, was Thomas William Parsons.

Beginning to write contemporaneously with the earliest American poets, at a time when only the veriest doggerel had yet been perpetrated in this country, he felt keenly the sense of isolation which it was the lot of men of letters in those days to experience — an isolation the reality of which the younger generation finds it difficult to appreciate. This is the excuse, though it is certainly not a justification, for the deprecatory and provincial tone which characterizes what are probably the earliest of his poems that have been preserved, the "Letters" which stand at the beginning of his first volume. Not Dickens himself was more flippantly scornful of America and the Americans than is Parsons in these "Letters;" and though in the preface to them he attributes the sentiments they contain to an imaginary "wandering Englishman," thus disclaiming them as personal, he shows even in doing so something more than a dramatic sympathy with the attitude they portray. This provincialism Parsons soon outgrew, but he never came to be in perfect touch with his country, nor to have that sense of easy security with regard to her which should mark the citizen of a nationality fully mature.

Yet even in these presumably juvenile verses there is much vigorous writing and some genuine humor. This on Boston, for example:

> " This town, in olden times of stake and flame,
> A famous nest of Puritans became :
> Sad, rigid souls, who hated as they ought
> The carnal arms wherewith the devil fought;
> Dancing and dicing, music, and whate'er
> Spreads for humanity the pleasing snare.
> Stage-plays, especially, their hearts abhorred,.
> Holding the muses hateful to the Lord,
> Save when old Sternhold and his brother bard
> Oped their hoarse throats, and strained an anthem hard.
> From that angelic race of perfect men
> (Sure, seraphs never trod the world till then!)
> Descends the race to whom the sway is given
> Of the world's morals by confiding Heaven."

There was always a strain of true religious feeling in Parsons, which deepened at the last into something rapt and intense; but Puritanism never ceased to be hateful to him, and this antagonism contributed to make him feel that his footsteps were on alien soil. An artist first of all, he was drawn more toward the services of the ancient Church, for whose adornment art has so bountifully poured out its treasures, than to any balder form of worship. To him the world was a problem in beauty and emotion. He was not incommoded with a message, as so many of his contemporaries were. This has been, perhaps, to the detriment of his reputation in the past; it may be to its advantage in the future. The man who speaks too consciously a message to his own time is apt to have none for any other. Parsons wrought from first to last in the true artistic spirit, and it is not un-likely that his chief claims to the recognition of the future will be found in qualities of form and style.

Not the least among these qualities will be that sturdy literary independence which, amid the widespread æsthetic revival of this century, achieved a success of a purely æsthetic nature on lines entirely unaffected by the contemporary fashion. In a time of metrical experiment, and of the new and strange harmonies of Rossetti and Swinburne, he alone of the artistic school of poets, uninfluenced even by Coleridge or Shelley, worked in the severe methods of an earlier day. Dryden and Pope seem to have been his earliest masters, but not for long. The versification of Dryden, which Keats learned to appreciate at its true value, remained always to some extent a factor in Parsons's art, but he soon threw over the jingle of Pope's measure for the fuller, statelier, and in truth simpler manner of Collins and Gray. Yet his matured style is neither that of Collins, with whom he had close resemblances, personal and poetical, nor that of Gray, though unquestionably akin to both. Parsons had, besides, a certain bent for plain words and homely images that sometimes became Dantesque. Indeed, the lifelong study which he gave to Dante could not be without its influence on his own expression — an influence potent for strength and directness.

Parsons was probably Gray's inferior in point of taste, for otherwise we can hardly understand how he could put forth in the same volume, and sometimes in the same poem, such inequalities as he permitted himself. Yet it must be said, as an offset to this, that he seldom made himself responsible for a poem by publishing it. He occasionally had verses in the magazines, and even, if the whim took him, in the newspapers; but only twice in his life did he bring the question of his critical judgment fairly within the scope of comment by issuing a volume to the public. The first of these volumes, which contains the famous " Lines on a Bust of Dante," may perhaps rely upon the youth of its author as an explanation of its unevenness. The other, " Circum Præcordia," published in the year of his death, and consisting of a versification of the collects of the Church together with a few original poems of a religious character, is of even and sustained excellence, though rising to the level of his best work only in its concluding poem, "Paradisi Gloria." Mrs. Parsons had several other volumes printed for private circulation only, but of these the author frequently knew nothing until the bound copies were placed in his hands. What he would himself now select to give to the world no one can tell; possibly as carefully edited a volume as even that of Gray.

Such a volume would, I believe, be one of the treasures of American verse — a book that lovers of poetry would carry with them as they would similar thin volumes of Herrick, Marvell, Collins or Landor. The lyrics addressed to Francesca are true Herrick for grace and daintiness, and there is nothing in Landor finer than such passages as this:

> " His heart was written o'er, like some stray page
> Torn out from Plutarch, with majestic names; "

or these, from " Francesca di Rimini : "

> " Be it some comfort, in that hateful hell,
> You had a lover of your love to tell."

> " But he whose numbers gave you unto fame,
> Lord of the lay — I need not speak his name —
> Was one who felt; whose life was love or hate.
> Born for extremes, he scorned the middle state,
> And well he knew that, since the world begun,
> The heart was master in the world of man."

I have referred to the " Paradisi Gloria." This poem, with one unwisely altered line restored to its original reading, is one of the few faultless lyrics in the language; and the following stanza, with which it begins, is, I submit, as felicitous as anything Gray ever wrote, and more imaginative;

> " There is a city builded by no hand,
> And unapproachable by sea or shore,
> And unassailable by any band
> Of storming soldiery forevermore."

Less fine, perhaps, but still very beautiful is the touching " Dirge : "

> " What shall we do now, Mary being dead?
> Or say or write, that shall express the half?
> What can we do but pillow that fair head,
> And let the springtime write her epitaph? "

Each of these poems is marked by that simple and straightforward style which was the glory of Parsons at his best. But he could also handle more involved periods and a more complex cæsural music with equal skill; witness the opening lines of " La Pineta Distrutta : "

> " Farewell Ravenna's forest! and farewell
> For aye through coming centuries to the sound,
> Over blue Adria of the lyric pines
> And Chiassi's bird-song keeping burden sweet
> To their low moan as once to Dante's lines,

> Which when my step first felt Italian ground
> I strove to follow, carried by the spell
> Of that sad Florentine **whose native street**
> (At morn **and** midnight) where he used to dwell
> My Father bade me pace with reverent feet."

From poems like these to "The Feud of the Flute-Players" **is a far cry,** but it argues well for the humanity of our poet that he could be merry when he would. The line,

> "In a tap-room by the Tiber, at the sign of Tarquin's Head,"

**is as jolly a bit of Bohemianism as any I** know, and the entire story **is told with much spirit and humor.** "St. Peray," another bacchanalian lyric, has found its way, like the "Lines on a Bust on Dante," into the anthologies, and may be passed by here with a mere reference.

"Count Ernst von Mansfeldt, the Protestant," if three rather weak and quite unnecessary stanzas could be removed **from it, would be,** perhaps, **the strongest poem Parsons ever wrote. It is** certainly the most **objective, and one of the most manly and** vigorous.

> "The dicer Death has flung for me;
>   His greedy eyes are on me;
> My chance is not one throw in three;
>   Ere night he will **have won me.**
>
> "Summon my kin! — come steed — come coach —
>   Let me not stay, commanding;
> If the last enemy approach,
>   They shall see me armed and standing.
>
> **"Buckle me well and belt me strong!**
>   **For I will fall in iron."**

This, **with the stirring** "Martial Ode," which begins,

> "Ancient of days! Thy prophets old
>   Declared Thee also Lord of war;
> And sacred chroniclers have told
>   Of kings whom Thou didst battle for,"

proves that Parsons knew how to put into practice that strenuous counsel of his own:

> " But something rough and resolute and sour
>    Should with the sweetness of the soul combine;
> For although gentleness be part of power,
>    'Tis only strength makes gentleness divine."

With the masterly technical power and equipment that Parsons undoubtedly had, why did he not do more? Why is his permanent original contribution to English literature limited to a few lyrics? For this I can find no better reason than that which I have already suggested, that, being out of sympathy with his time, he found no theme for his song. The achievements of this age he admired, when at all, as an outsider, and frequently his attitude was the reverse of admiration. Homers must have their Agamemnons as well as Agamemnons their Homers; and to-day was not heroic to Parsons. To him the railway suggested nothing but

> " The dead sleepers of the vulgar track,"

and commercial greatness smacked ever of the Philistine. He would probably have been as uncomfortable in Athens as in Boston; and while he could love Venice dead, Venice living (where, as so often in history, Trade and Art went out hand in hand, conquering and to conquer) would have been as distasteful as Chicago. It is true that the traders of Athens and the Adriatic braved great personal dangers, and brought back from their voyages strange and gorgeous fabrics, " barbaric pearl and gold," and tales of incredible adventure in the unknown world. Our modern conquests, in commerce as in science, with some notable exceptions, are of a more impalpable kind, and make no such sensuous appeal to the imagination. And so, for some, the circumnavigation of the globe has ended all romance, even though the unknown be still as mysteriously present in New York as in the "shining vales of Har."

The risk and the imagination involved in modern achievement are enormous, and even the element of personal danger is by no means eliminated; and if there were vulgar things in the conquest of California, I doubt not there were also vulgar things, more nearly of the same kind than we are apt to think, in the conquest of Gaul. But anybody can see the

vulgarity. It is the poet's function to show that this is a
mere accident, and that the essential reality still throbs as
ever with a lyric rapture; that

> " in the mud and scum of things
> There's something ever, ever sings."

Few poets, indeed, have been completely catholic of insight, nor do they necessarily lose their title of interpreters
because they are not universal interpreters, and limit themselves to the field or fields for which they have a spontaneous
sympathy. Parsons, even when he rationally approved, had
no spontaneous sympathy for the present, its attitude or its
tendencies. To sing of it, or to sing of the past with the
voice of the present, his æsthetic instinct felt would be
but a *tour de force*, and seldom and reluctantly was he per-
suaded to attempt it. Occasionally he poured his fine rheto-
ric into denunciation, written from the heart; but here, too,
his artistic feeling stepped in and restrained him to brief
utterance, for he knew well that scolding is not great nor
dignified.

One thing there was that he saw clearly his way to do —
to reproduce for this age the voice of the age which he did
love, and of the poet for whom, even from boyhood, he
cherished a devotion almost personal. In making this choice
and following his instinct, I believe he was right, and that
we have obtained a greater poem than we should have done
had he forced himself into attempting a sustained work of
his own. Nor is this a derogation in any way from Parsons's
unquestioned poetic power, as any one who knows anything
about the almost insuperable difficulties of translation is well
aware. In fact, it may be said with perfect truth that a
good translation is rarer than a good original poem. The
successful transfer of even the briefest lyric from one
language to another is an achievement so unusual as to de-
mand the most unreserved commendation, while even the
partly successful renderings of the great masters, in all
languages, are so few that their names may be spoken in
one breath.

Parsons's translation of the " Divine Comedy" is far from

being a paraphrase of the original, but yet it makes no pretense to absolute literalness. Indeed, a truly literal translation is a linguistic impossibility. Over and above the merely metrical difficulties of such an undertaking, there must always be two classes of phenomena in which the two poems, the original and the version, will differ, and often very materially, from each other. The metrical scheme may be preserved, but the rhythmical filling in of this scheme must necessarily vary; for the syllables of the corresponding words in different languages will almost certainly have different time values. In one they may have many consonants, and be perforce slow in articulation; in the other they may consist entirely of short vowels and tripping liquids. The predominance of short syllables in Italian enabled Dante to use feet of three or more syllables in an iambic measure with much greater frequency than would be possible in English, and this fact alters wholly the character of a measure of which the metrical scheme is the same in both languages. It is, of course, so evident as hardly to warrant allusion that the sounds themselves cannot be the same; and yet their expression as mere sounds is a very vital factor in their poetic force.

The other class of phenomena in which an original and its translation must always differ is not acoustic, but linguistic. As I have had occasion to say elsewhere, " words differ in what, for lack of a better word, we must call color. With the possible exception of Volapük, in which, for this very reason, no one but a statistician would ever think of writing poetry, there is no language in existence in which the words are merely conventional symbols of the ideas for which they stand. Every word we speak has a pedigree that goes back to Adam. It has been developing into what it now is, through uncounted accretions and curtailments and transformations, ever since man was, and, since Professor Garner's experiments with monkeys, we may suspect even a little longer; and in the course of that long, eventful history it has gathered to itself a multitude of little associations which, without presenting themselves directly to the understanding, modify, enrich and color the effect of the primary meaning, like the overtones of a musical note. Without this colorific value of words, we could express little more by speech than by the symbols of algebra. This is the chief difficulty of the translator, and one that he can never surmount."

Prose translations of what in the original was verse vary, of course, from that original in even more respects, since they deliberately sacrifice an entire group of expressional devices which formed an important part of the poet's intention. An argument may be made for the use of prose in translating the poetry of the ancients, for their versification differed from ours in a radical manner. But there can be no excuse for an English prose version of a poem written in any modern European language, if it be intended for more than an assistance in the study of the original. Admirable as the workmanship in some of our prose versions of Dante has been, I cannot but think that, except for some such scholarly purpose, the labor and the skill expended upon them have been misapplied.

At the opposite extreme from the prose versions are those that have been made into *terza rima*. It cannot be denied that the use of Dante's own arrangement of rhymes is an advantage, nor that Dante himself laid much stress upon it. But he had mystical reasons for doing so that are not of great consequence to us now, and Parsons's translation, while preserving, in common with the versions in *terza rima* and with those in blank verse, the meter of the original (the iambic pentameter), loses but little of the effect of the rhyme structure. His quatrains, by the liberal use of run-on lines and the occasional introduction of a third rhyme, achieve that effect of continuity which is the most distinguishing characteristic of the original. I venture to think that almost no one, even among poets, would be able to tell whether the complex rhyme system of the *terza rima* were exactly carried out in any poem to the reading aloud of which he should listen for pure enjoyment, and without special effort to observe that particular phenomenon. Still, however slight the advantage be, it is nevertheless an advantage to have preserved the *terza rima*; but this gain is more than overcome by the Dantesque quality of the style in Parsons's version. The manner of the others often suggests the contemporaries of Dante, rather than Dante himself.

There remain for consideration and comparison the two renderings into blank verse. These are the most widely known of the various translations, and one of them, Cary's, is the form in which Dante is most generally read by English-speaking readers. Longfellow's version, though occasionally it transfers a line more successfully than any of the others, is in the main perfunctory, and its literalness is carried so far that it frequently degenerates into a "crib" pure and simple. There is a story that Longfellow used to translate eighty lines every morning before breakfast. I do not know how true this may be, but the internal evidence seems to support it. The product of his labor is a *caput mortuum*; the categorical statements are all there, but somehow the poetry has evaporated. The result is tedious and uninteresting. Now, the one quality Dante never had is dullness, and that is also the one quality the public will never forgive.

Cary's translation has the merit of being tolerably readable. But in it the great Italian poet suffers a strange transformation. The words are the words of Dante, but the voice is the voice of Milton; or rather of a weaker-lunged man trying to mouth the mighty periods and cæsuras of Milton, and getting somewhat cracked of voice and broken of wind in the effort. Nevertheless, it is, on the whole, a creditable performance; only it is not Dante.

Each of the translators has his felicitous moments, and succeeds in rendering certain passages with more skill than his competitors. But the relative merit of the translations must be estimated, not by passages, but by the general impression of the whole work. Parsons is inferior to some of the other translators in certain obvious verbal and prosodical accuracies. But his poem probably gives a more correct impression of Dante in his entirety than any of the others. His versification has the continuity of Dante's, and something of its music. His diction, like Dante's, has that supreme refinement that knows no disdain for homely words and phrases. His style, with more inversions than Dante's, has much of the master's severity and swiftness, though it falls short of the masterfulness and supple power of the Italian. Altogether there is more Dante in it than in any translation that has yet been made.

It has been difficult for me to write critically of a man for whom I had a warm affection, and who honored me with his friendship and esteem. If I have erred on the side of severity, it has been from a fear lest my personal regard for the man should unduly influence my judgment of the poet; and if I have erred in his praise, it will be easily forgiven. But I do not think that I mistake in assigning to him, as a translator a station with the highest, and as an original poet a niche with Collins in the temple of English song.

RICHARD HOVEY.

*In Atlantic Monthly.*

www.ingramcontent.com/pod-product-compliance
Lightning Source LLC
Chambersburg PA
CBHW031929060726
47496CB00008BA/2781